PRAISE FC

CU00969728

'It figures he'd come from a place called Pringles, where
funny music resounds and nothing ever happens, except
everything . . . Beauty and dark truth flow through his work . . .
I once met Aira at a writer's conference in Denmark. I was so
excited at his presence that I bounded his way like a St. Bernard,
but once I reached him all I could think to say – channeling
my inner Chris Farley – was that he was awesome.'

Patti Smith

'If there is one contemporary writer who defies classification, it
is César Aira. His novels seem to put the theories of Gombrowicz
into practice, except, and the difference is fundamental, that
Gombrowicz was the abbot of a luxurious imaginary monastery,
while Aira is a nun or novice among the Discalced Carmelites of
the Word. Sometimes he is reminiscent of Roussel (Roussel on
his knees in a bath red with blood), but the only living writer to
whom he can be compared is Barcelona's Enrique Vila-Matas.'

Roberto Bolaño

'Aira is firmly in the tradition of Jorge Luis Borges and W. G. Sebald.'

Mark Doty, *Los Angeles Times*

'Aira's works are like slim cabinets of wonder, full of unlikely
juxtapositions. His unpredictability is masterful.'

Rivka Galchen

'Aira is one of the most provocative and idiosyncratic novelists
working in Spanish today, and should not be missed.'

New York Times Book Review

THE LITTLE BUDDHIST MONK

THE LITTLE BUDDHIST MONK

César Aira

Translated by
Nick Caistor

SHEFFIELD – LONDON

First published in 2017 by And Other Stories
Sheffield – London
www.andotherstories.org

Originally published in Spanish by Editorial Mansalva, Buenos Aires, in 2005 as
El Pequeño Monje Budista.

9 8 7 6 5 4 3 2 1

ISBN 978-1-908276-98-8
eBook ISBN 978-1-908276-99-5

Editors: Luke Brown and Tara Tobler; Proofreader: Sarah Terry; Typesetter: Tetragon,
London; Typefaces: Linotype Swift Neue and Verlag; Cover Design: Edward Bettison;
Printed and bound by TJ International Ltd, Padstow, Cornwall, UK.

A catalogue record for this book is available from the British Library.

This work was published within the framework of the Sur Translation Support
Program of the Ministry of Foreign Affairs, International Trade and Worship of
the Argentine Republic. Obra editada en el marco del Programa "Sur" de Apoyo a
las Traducciones del Ministerio de Relaciones Exteriores y Culto de la República
Argentina.

This book was also supported using public funding by Arts Council England.

Supported using public funding by

**ARTS COUNCIL
ENGLAND**

MIX
Paper from
responsible sources
FSC® C013056

THE LITTLE BUDDHIST MONK

I

A little Buddhist monk was anxious to emigrate from his native land, which was none other than Korea. He wanted to go to Europe or America. The project had been incubating in his brain from his youth, almost since infancy, and had coloured his entire life. At the age when other children were exploring the world about them, he was discovering a longing for distant worlds, and what he saw around him seemed like the misleading image of a reality that awaited on the other side of the planet. He didn't really remember, but he could have sworn that even before he knew of Europe or America, he already wanted to go, as if he had been programmed within to receive the calls of faraway places. At any rate, his ignorance, if that is what it was, did not last long, because his earliest reading was geographical; later on, studying the cultures of the countries he dreamed of took up more of his time than his religious training, which in the order he belonged to was extremely demanding. Intelligent and obstinate despite his diminutive size, he enjoyed a distinguished career as a monk while at night he studied languages, history, philosophy, politics and psychoanalysis, in addition to reading Shakespeare, Balzac, Kafka and anything else worthwhile. Our little Buddhist monk was living proof of the saying: 'Knowledge takes up no space.'

Of course, this intellectual preparation only solved half the problem, and the second half at that; the first part, that of practicalities, remained unresolved. To start with, there was no real possibility of saving the money he needed for the airfare. And over there, in the dreamt-of First World, he didn't know anyone who could find him a job to support himself. More seriously still, he had no idea of what kind of work this might be. He was not equipped for any kind of profession, at least not a conventional one. He was not unaware that every so often Buddhism became fashionable in one or other of the western countries, or in all of them at once; and he knew that the people in those countries most likely to follow these fashions were members of the well-heeled classes. They would pay handsomely for a genuine article like the little Buddhist monk. In fact, he knew of quite a few compatriots who had successfully exploited that seam. But they had done so as part of institutions that organised the journey, accompanied them, installed them and lent them legitimacy. Unfortunately, the order he belonged to was extremely localised; it did nothing to promote itself, was against teaching outside the group and detested all institutional organisations. So much so that it was a misuse of language to say that he 'belonged' to the order, since once they had completed their studies, its members were left to their own devices, without teachers, monasteries or rules. They were wandering mendicant monks or, if they so wished, they were sedentary, public preachers of independent means; in short, they could be whatever they wished without anyone holding them to account. They had no way of recognising one another. It was possible that they were all equally determined to emigrate but didn't know it, and each believed he was the only one. It was possible they were all equally reduced in stature like the little Buddhist monk, but didn't know that either.

To have a project can help make life liveable, and it doesn't matter how madcap and unattainable it might be; quite the opposite, in fact, because if that is the case, its influence will be all the more absorbing and prolonged. Practical people say that dreams serve no purpose; but they can't deny that at least they allow one to dream. The dream of a journey had endowed the little Buddhist's life with meaning. Without it, his existence would have been lost in the capricious inconsequentiality of contemporary Korean history and, tiny as he was, his efforts would have been wasted. Thanks to the project, all his studies and readings complemented one another; none was wasted. Someone might ask: what do studying Hegel, reading Truman Capote, poring over the plans of the châteaux of the Loire and delving into the struggles for power between Guelphs and Ghibellines, Tories and Whigs, Republicans and Democrats have in common? These might seem fragments of disparate areas of knowledge, and in anybody else they would indeed have simply fed a pointless curiosity. In him, they were all directed towards a common goal. Practically no leap of his agile mind, whatever discipline he applied it to, failed to contribute to his ultimate goal. In a word, the project had given his life its orientation, and if it seems unnecessary for someone in the Orient to find orientation in this way, just imagine that if the Orient exists, it is because on the other side there is the Occident, and it was precisely this that caused the little Buddhist monk so many sleepless nights.

But one day his dream would come true, he thought, as he raised his eyes to the sky in which he glimpsed the distant reflection of the skies awaiting him. 'It costs nothing to dream,' he told himself. And if reality was defined by its identification with itself, he glimpsed in that inverted overlap of antipodean skies the triumphant congruence of dreams and life.

II

The escape route presented itself unexpectedly one day in the shape of a French photographer who was visiting Korea. As well as being unexpected, it was extraordinarily casual, as the vagaries of fate tend to be. Lost in his daydreams outside a luxury hotel, the little Buddhist monk was almost knocked over by a couple who were suddenly spat out by the revolving door. With a rapid manoeuvre – a leap to one side and two or three hasty steps – he managed to avoid being trampled on. He was accustomed to this kind of dodge: a sixth sense warned him of the danger, while his strolls through the busiest parts of the city produced such a plethora of these incidents that they became a constant weaving from one side to another. His tiny stature meant that not everyone saw him, but even if they did, it wasn't easy for them to calculate the consequences of their respective movements, since one step for a pedestrian of normal size was equivalent to five from the little Buddhist monk.

The man and woman who emerged from the hotel were extra large. He was fat and as tall as a basketball player. He was weighed down by a capacious backpack, climber's boots, trousers patched with a multitude of stuffed pockets, and a jacket that gave away his profession. She was scarcely less big, with ash-blonde hair, horsey features, red hands and thin lips that failed completely to conceal the braces on her protruding teeth. She was wearing an elegant man's suit. From the summit of their corpulence they did not even spot the presence of the little being they had been on the point of crushing, and they would have left him behind in a second if they hadn't altered course and headed for the kerb. From their gestures it was plain they wished to hail a taxi. Had it not been for this change of direction, which obliged the little Buddhist monk to take evasive action a second time, he would have returned at once to his daydreams and continued on his way, further repeating his jumps and accelerations through the crowds. And he would have done so anyway, if at that very moment one of the couple had not uttered part of a sentence in a language he knew. The words were, I quote: '*quelqu'un qui parle français*', which doubtless referred to their debate about which taxi to take. They must have wanted (how naïve!) to be driven by someone who spoke their language.

Then, before the story could resume its fluid course of events, there was one final moment when chance had to choose between what did happen and what might have happened. If the little Buddhist monk had thought about it for an instant, if his mind had even fleetingly taken into account his timidity, his insignificance, or the general pointlessness of everything, he would not have opened his mouth. But as this was not the case, he pronounced the words that complemented what he had heard: '*Moi, je parle français.*' He failed to realise that what he had heard might only be part of the proposition. 'Someone who speaks French' could be the conclusion of a phrase along the lines of: 'Let's hope we don't have the misfortune to bump into someone who speaks French.' Which only goes to prove that sometimes it's better not to think.

When the French couple heard this unexpected but fitting reply, they were taken aback. They must have thought for a moment that they were faced with a supernatural phenomenon, which they could have put down to the immanent magic of Korea. It is only natural that tourists, especially when they travel really far, lose all sense of proportion in their expectations, or are content to set out with a delicious, tantalising vagueness, as if to allow the possibility that the strangest things could happen. And to a European, the furthest East is naturally a world of enchantment. This moment lasted rather longer than it should have, because when they peered around, they could not see a soul. Had the voice come from somewhere inside themselves, from the mystery of their marriage? The lack of an accent added to their doubts. When they finally spotted the little Buddhist monk they smiled and greeted him, still rather shocked.

This tiny incident was the beginning of a mutually beneficial relationship. The little Buddhist monk immediately sensed that his opportunity had arrived. But the opportunity for what? In a flash, as if he were about to be hit by a train, he saw it all. A rich French traveller (it was a luxury hotel), for whom he could act as a guide, show him his worth, become his irreplaceable assistant, and by means of subtle diplomacy, win the favour of being taken with him . . . Beyond that, which was no more than a spark of his imagination, was the life he would lead in Paris, the fire this spark would ignite. He was astonished. It was as though it was only at this moment that the project to emigrate was born, and it exploded with such force that it gave a retrospective glow to all his previous life, endowing it with a meaning that until now it had lacked.

III

The first and most important consequence of this chance conversation by the pavement's edge was that the French couple gave up on their idea of taking a taxi. Because they had to admit they didn't have any precise destination, or rather they did have one but did not know where to find it (this obscure point was soon cleared up). The apparition of this 'providential man', as they called him, even though they recognised that the phrase sounded strange when applied to someone so tiny, spared them this unnecessary wandering.

They discovered that they had lots to say to each other, far too much to remain standing there buffeted by the flood of people crowding the street at that time of day. After some hesitation, they invited him to a cafe: on the one hand they were uncertain whether as a monk he was allowed to enter this kind of establishment, and on the other they did not know whether in Korea there were cafes where people could sit and chat (they had only just arrived). On a more subliminal level, their doubts also sprang from a fear of offending him, since as a result of the difference in their height, when they spoke to him standing up they had to lean forward, and it might seem very impolite to invite him to sit down simply to be level with him and avoid a backache. By then, after the initial exchange of pleasantries, they considered him too valuable to offend in any way. They had only just met him, and were already afraid of losing him.

The little Buddhist monk swept aside these fears at a stroke when he said that of the many cafes they could choose from in the neighbourhood, he recommended one that was just round the corner. They went straight there. It really was very close. As they entered, the French couple admired the decor; they thought it was very like *Les Deux Magots*. The same dark wood panelling, the old leather chairs, the partitions with bevelled glass, the shiny brass. At that time of morning there were few customers. They ordered coffee, and began to talk.

The Frenchman was called Napoleon Chirac. He was a freelance photographer: he didn't work for any agency, and did not accept commissions. He regarded himself more as an artist than a conventional photographer. His camera had taken him around the world, from Australia to Canada, according to his whims or his inspiration.

While he didn't avoid the exotic, it was not the focus of his searches; on the contrary, he explored the exotic in order to reveal its ordinariness.

An image hunter? asked the little Buddhist monk.

Not exactly. However odd it might seem, images were not his objective, or were only a by-product. His work was with spaces.

Spaces? What did he mean? And how could one speak of spaces in the plural, when space itself was one, a single, continuous and all-embracing whole?

He was referring to human spaces, or rather the way that different cultures compartmentalised space. For example, the alleys of New York, the museums in the Old World, football stadiums . . .

The list could have been endless. The little Buddhist monk gave in to the temptation to demonstrate his wit, despite knowing full well that wit always runs the risk of being excessive or inappropriate. But this time he hit the spot:

Dolls' houses?

Napoleon smiled and looked at his wife. No, he had not tried with dolls' houses. It hadn't occurred to him, perhaps because it would be difficult with his method of working. 'Difficult', but not 'impossible'. He would have to use a special lens. It might be worth the effort.

This observation led to a momentary change of topic. The little Buddhist monk had proved so intelligent that the two foreigners' attention turned to him. And since they found it impossible to ask why he was so intelligent, they questioned him about something as close as possible to that: how had he come to speak such perfect French? Had he lived in France?

This was a good opportunity for him to express his desire to emigrate, and yet he preferred to leave that for another occasion; he was certain there would be one. For the moment, the little Buddhist monk responded with a white lie: he said he had taken conversation classes at the Alliance Française. Then he cleverly redirected the conversation back to its previous course, taking up again a point that had been mentioned but not elaborated on: what was the Frenchman's 'method of working'?

It consisted in photographing a 'space' from its centre, covering the whole perimeter in a series of linked images. Then he made a digital 'join' which produced one single landscape-format photograph.

The little Buddhist monk nodded. He understood. It was ingenious, although it might not be all that original; he thought he had seen something similar, if not the same, in an art magazine. But he didn't say this. Napoleon Chirac was opening the backpack he had placed on the bench beside him. He took out an oblong box about sixty centimetres by twenty, and began to lay the photos in it on to the table.

He explained that this was his latest project: dance halls in Havana. Recalling his earlier explanation, it was not hard to interpret them, but even so they had a strangeness about them that made them interesting. The montage of the different pictures was perfect. What they showed were empty salons, some of them with tables and chairs, a piano, or a platform or stage, a bar, doors, windows. At first glance the image looked like a single photograph taken with a wide-angle lens, but closer observation revealed distortions in the perspective and besides, it became obvious that the shot was too wide. The left- and right-hand edges coincided at exactly the same point; if either picture had been even a few centimetres longer, there would have been a repetition, and although this would have made reading the image easier, it would also have revealed the trick.

Napoleon showed him a dozen or more of these images. They were in colour, and printed on very glossy paper; the dance halls, some of them bigger than others (although it was hard to tell), were sordid and sad, contrasting sharply with the strange air of luxury lent by the mechanism of straightening out the circular shape. None had any people in them. The little Buddhist monk asked if this was a deliberate choice always.

Which indeed it was, in all the series. Only when there was no piece of furniture to suggest the human scale did he introduce an isolated figure to suggest the dimensions . . . At this point there was a short silence, one of those polite pauses the French couple would have to get used to with an interlocutor of the unusual size that they had stumbled across.

Well, then: after the Havana dance halls, he had wondered: now what? And decided . . .

One moment. Forgive the interruption, but how did he choose the themes? Because after all, there were 'spaces' everywhere. Without needing to quote Pascal and the 'miseries of mankind' that came from 'the impossibility of man of staying at home along in a quiet room', it had to be recognised that the house one lives in is also a 'space'.

Yes, that was true, but the idea was to explore culturally charged spaces. And the photographer's vocation had always been that of a traveller. How did he choose his subjects? As he had already said, whim and chance were part of it. He found his subjects through reading, films, TV documentaries. Sometimes he just set off on an impulse, or went in search of one thing and discovered something different.

What about now? Why Korea?

His current project involved Korea's Buddhist temples.

On hearing this, the little Buddhist monk raised his eyebrows. He thought for a while, glanced at the long photographs spread over the table, thought about it again, and nodded. Napoleon Chirac smiled, relieved and content. With good reason: it was important to him to get the approval of an intelligent local who after only the briefest explanation had understood what he was trying to do.

I have to warn you, said the little Buddhist monk, that the temples you're going to find here are not enclosed spaces.

The Frenchman already knew this. On this occasion it was not a random voyage, although every trip had something unexpected about it that made it worthwhile. He had done his research, and this openness of Korean Buddhism to nature was the challenge that had led to his choice.

Did he have a particular temple or temples in mind?

He took a tourist map of the country out of his backpack and unfolded it. He showed him photographs of the temples of Bulguksa, Sinheungsa and others.

What do you think of them?

There are other less touristy ones. If you will allow me, I could guide you.

This was what the French couple had been hoping for, and they leapt at the offer:

Seriously? Would you be so kind? It would be such an invaluable help to us. Would you have the time to spare? Won't it interfere with your duties?

I have absolutely nothing to do. And even if I did, I could think of no better use of my time than to serve an eminent artist and to enjoy the company of an educated, delightful foreign couple with whom I can practise my poor French.

Many thanks. How kind. We ought to agree on adequate financial compensation . . .

Not at all! he interrupted the Frenchman. I'll do it for the pleasure and honour of doing so. This is where the sacred duties of hospitality and the most elementary patriotism coincide. Besides, the order I belong to forbids me to receive any emoluments. I don't know if you noticed, but my apparel doesn't have any pockets.

The French couple were delighted. They couldn't believe their luck. The little fellow was giant-sized.

IV

To celebrate they ordered a bottle of champagne. No one could deny it was worth it, because they really did have something to celebrate. Even so they hesitated for a few moments, because they were aware that drinking champagne in the morning was a bold statement. When asked, the little Buddhist monk declared that he had no objection to alcoholic beverages. And among these, rather than a cheap sherry or a run-of-the-mill whisky, Napoleon Chirac, to whom the choice had been left, was inclined towards what was after all most logical. Champagne had the exact symbolic resonance that the moment called for, and was appropriate above and beyond the symbolic, since it was a good aperitif; and besides, it was no longer that early in the day.

But when they raised their glasses in a toast, the French couple froze in surprise. The 'clink' of the glass captured a snapshot of their astonishment. The only things moving were the tiny bubbles inside the glasses, and it was precisely these bubbles that were the object of the foreigners' rapt attention: instead of rising, they descended, going from the surface of the liquid to the bottom, where they fizzed about in crazy swirls.

By now entirely assuming his role as a national guide, the little Buddhist monk dismissed the supposed miracle with a laugh. Instead he gave a perfectly rational explanation: they should not forget that they were on the far side of the world, and the magnetic poles were reversed.

In addition, he went on, as they sipped their drinks, in general Korea had something of the 'world upside down' about it. Not so much in its practical, visible aspects as in certain mental structures. In fact, the country's modernisation that followed from contact with western travellers and traders in the sixteenth century had been the by-product of a religious polemic that had its roots in a strange inversion.

The French couple drank in his words. His French was so perfect and elegant it sounded pre-recorded. Encouraged by their close attention, he explained:

The conflict had arisen between two branches of Buddhism who were arguing about the way to tell jokes. One of them, innovatory thanks to western influence (and which ultimately was triumphant), proposed telling them with the punchline at the end. The other school resisted any change, and defended the traditional

Korean way of telling them, in which the punchline or climax should come at the beginning, not the end.

An example? Of course. The innovators proposed:

I have no legs. I'm a snake.

Whereas the traditionalists argued in favour of the ancient way, one that had made so many generations laugh:

I'm a snake. I have no legs.

The little Buddhist monk readily admitted that this example might not help clarify things much. It was not for nothing that one of the two schools of thought had won out, and for centuries had shaped the mental categories that were part and parcel of the perception of the joke. From the vantage point of the present it was hard to understand the virulence of the passions aroused by this debate. One had to take into account the force of habit, and the ancestral creation of expectations. That was what it was about: the role of people's expectations. What also needed to be taken into account was that the controversy took place in a religious context, so that jokes were not jokes in the modern sense, but parables with a spiritual significance.

However, the undisputed, complete triumph of the modernising school, which gave Korea its place in the modern world, had not led to the disappearance or forgetting of the ancient way. On the contrary, its persistence as a mental substratum was what made jokes funny.

How strange all this is, said Napoleon Chirac. It gives one such a strong impression of having left the normal world behind and of being on the far side of the looking-glass.

The little Buddhist monk responded to this with a conciliatory smile: it wasn't that big a deal. Globalisation, so reviled by nationalists of every stripe, had led to greater communication, which meant that previously unnoticed inversions were lent greater contrast and meaning.

Korea, he said, had not only taken but given. A great exporter of products with high added value and cutting-edge technology, it had become respected throughout the world as the supplier of the most demanding consumer goods. And it has also exported a valuable human resource, in the substantial emigration of a disciplined, hard-working labour force, enterprising traders, small business owners (and big ones) who have established their picturesque Korean neighbourhoods in every city around the world.

And, turning to a specific point that might interest them, Korea also exported art. From the most serious kind, the art of museums, of which one eminent example was Nam June Paik, whose work they surely knew (they nodded) to the most popular forms of entertainment such as the amusing cartoon of SpongeBob SquarePants.

Was SpongeBob SquarePants Korean? They thought it was American.

It was true that now it was promoted by a North American company, but it was created in Korea, and was in fact a typical Korean creation. It still bore traces of that even after the distortions it had suffered at the hands of western cartoonists.

Moreover, he went on, in the genesis of SpongeBob SquarePants there was an echo of the old controversy about jokes. Did they know what the cartoon was about? It shows the adventures of a boy sponge and his friends the starfish, the squid, the crab who owns a fast-food restaurant, the little diver squirrel . . . Well, the original idea was to have this character live either on the bottom of the sea, which is the natural habitat for sponges, or in a bathroom, in the little porcelain niche above the tub where human beings interact with sponges. In this latter case, it would have been an example of the traditional kind of joke from Korean folklore, with the resolution coming before the development. However, due to pressure from the North American TV channels, the other format was adopted, with the result that the climax of the joke would have to come at the end (the logical end) of a vast poetic saga that was both almost infinite and also very convenient from the commercial point of view.

The French couple were fascinated by this torrent of information, of which their tiny friend seemed to be an inexhaustible source. Since by now they had emptied the bottle, they ordered another one, and took advantage of the pause to change subjects. Napoleon Chirac picked up the tourist guide that had been left on the table and opened it in the middle once more, at the pages devoted to the famous temple at Bulguksa, a standout tourist attraction with three stars.

So you are of the opinion, he said, that it's not worth a visit to Bulguksa? Won't the series be incomplete without it?

Of course you must go there! exclaimed the little Buddhist monk. Of course the series would not be complete without the supreme diadem of the treasures of our Korean temples! What I said was that there are others which are more interesting because they are less well-known or celebrated. But Bulguksa is a must, it's unavoidable, like the Eiffel Tower or Times Square.

And in fact, he went on, Bulguksa had successfully withstood tourist vulgarisation. It could make a good subject for his photography, especially sectors such as the platform of the main shrine in the complex, Daeungjeon, where the two famous pagodas were placed.

The shrine was built in the second half of the eighth century by a prime minister, Kim Daeseoing, who was a follower of Buddhism. He had the two temples built in memory of his parents, and this could explain the differences between them if it was true, as tradition had it, that one was dedicated to the father, and the other to the mother. They are placed symmetrically on both sides of the square, though all the charm comes from their lack of symmetry, because they are very different to each other. The 'motherly' or 'feminine' pagoda, called Seokgatap, is the lower of the two (8.3 metres) and the simpler. It has three levels, and is elegant and austere. The name Seokgatap means 'the pagoda of Sakyamuni', the historical founder of Buddhism. Its construction represents the spiritual ascension following the rules imposed by the Buddha Sakyamuni. The symbolic idea is that this ascension is relatively easy if one adheres to the dogma. And perhaps it also means that this is the path recommended for women, who should not concern themselves with any great intellectual complexities but pursue the established rules obediently.

The other pagoda is called Dagotap, which means the 'Pagoda of a Thousand Treasures'. It is taller (10.5 metres), more solid and much more elaborate, with eaves, cornices, balustrades, doors and windows. Its baroque style symbolises the complexity of the world, whose 'thousand treasures' are mankind's ambition.

There exists a legend about these two pagodas that might interest you, said the little Buddhist monk.

Of course it would. The more he spoke, the more interested they became. This was both automatic and inevitable: had this not been the case, if their interests had already existed separately from each other and had to collide, it could never have happened. It would be like the Buddhist tale of the turtle that sleeps on the sea floor and swims up only once every hundred years. It can appear anywhere on the immense surface of the oceans, while also somewhere in that vastness floats a ring that is ten centimetres in diameter. What probability is there that, as it pops up, the turtle's head will pass through that ring? How long will one have to wait before that coincidence occurs? Just as unlikely are the odds of saying something to coincide with the interests of the person to whom one speaks. (The modern version of this turtle is Sponge-Bob SquarePants.)

The legend says that one morning a dead horse appeared in the square of Daeungjeon. It was flattened against the floor tiles, its spine crushed, skull smashed and brains spattered all around. It had obviously fallen from a great height, which explained the noise heard shortly before dawn by the monks now gathered crestfallen around the carcass. In their semi-conscious state they had thought that part of the temple had collapsed, but the Buddha sent them so many dreams at that time of morning that they had preferred to stay in bed.

The monks knew the dead animal. It was an imported Chinese pony that was tired of life and wanted to commit suicide. Its lack of knowledge of Korean botany meant it could not find the toxic herbs that could have brought its existence to a discreet end, and so instead it decided to throw itself into the void from the highest point it could climb to. In the region, there was nothing higher than the two pagodas at Daeungjeon. But how could it reach the top? It's not easy for anyone, still less a horse, to climb the outside of a steep building, to practise architectural rock-climbing. One has to realise the importance in Buddhism of the number of legs each living being has: an importance even greater in this case. With two legs (man, partridges) the climb would not have presented any great problem; with many (a centipede) even less; with four, it was mission impossible! Despite this, the horse's determination to end it all was so great that it set off on the climb. It chose the Seokgatap, which although it was slightly lower seemed to present fewer obstacles. It was an infinitely demanding task. Clinging desperately to the cornices, its hooves slipping everywhere, its round belly dangling to one side and its haunches to the other, in a clumsy imitation of Spiderman, climbing one centimetre and sliding back three, head down, curling up into a ball, folding and unfolding like an electrician's stepladder, the horse sweated and panted upwards for hour after hour. The monks recalled having heard during the night an irregular series of scraping sounds, thuds and snorting; they had attributed this to a flock of storks mating in the temple roofs.

Finally the desperate pony reached the top of the pagoda, and without giving it a second thought launched itself into the air. As it fell, at that supreme moment when everything was already decided, it saw it had made a mistake, and that rather than scaling the Seokgatap it had climbed the Dagotap. Instead of making things easy for itself, it had made them difficult. And during the instant of the fall it had time to reproach itself for this lack of attention, and to think that perhaps it was this failing that had led it to despair of life.

What a beautiful, sad story, the French couple commented, and what a rich message it must surely contain for anyone who can correctly interpret it.

V

They had been talking so much that the morning had sped by and, whether it was because they wanted an excuse to continue their conversation sitting down without having to start work, or because the champagne really had worked as an aperitif and had opened their appetite, the French couple suggested they have lunch together. They did so tentatively, admitting they did not know at what time Koreans ate, or more importantly, what plan of action the little man might have devised, since they had tacitly left it up to him.

Amply justifying their decision, the little Buddhist monk took charge. Yes, it made sense to go and eat, and to have a good lunch so that they could devote the whole afternoon to photography. He had already decided on the temple where the distinguished visitor could make his first foray: one that was in the vicinity of the city, easily accessible by train, not often visited but very characteristic.

They at once paid and left. The little Buddhist monk hurried along in front of them, saying he knew a nice place close by where the food was good and there was no problem getting a table. He set off through pedestrianised alleyways, and the French couple followed without losing sight of him, admiring the ease with which he slipped through the crowd of people who could not even see him. Although they paid close attention, they were always on the point of losing him, because he was rushing along so quickly at ground level, and so many people kept getting in their way. This pursuit gave them little time to see where they were going, but that was not important anyway, as they would never have been able to get their bearings: the narrow alleys became a real labyrinth. They turned to the right, then to the left, then right again, while at the same time the streets also turned right and left; they crossed roofed-in sections, one of which housed a bookshop, turned left and right again, and there they were. A set of very worn marble stairs led to a creaking glass door through which they entered before they could even glance at the front of the building or the signs outside, which they could not have read anyway.

It turned out to be a Greek restaurant, not a Korean one. The owner greeted them effusively and led them to a table. Only when they were finally seated did they get the chance to look around. They found themselves in a squarish room that was higher than it was wide, with about twenty tables covered in white paper cloths, heavy china plates, tin utensils and chunky glasses. Dark wooden beams stretched across the ceiling, and hanging from them, defiantly incoherent, were a great many crystal chandeliers. None of them was lit; what little light there was came in through the front window from the narrow street outside. The walls were lime-washed blue, with several small, garish oil paintings hanging from them.

Curious as all this was, it was nothing compared to the owner. He was a hyperactive, loud, middle-aged Greek with a very dark complexion, intensely black curly hair, thick eyebrows, sideburns and moustache, and a check shirt with the buttonholes bulging across his paunch. Even though there were two waiters, he busied himself at every table, shouted out all the orders, and when there weren't any, sang snatches of Italian opera in a deep voice that made the air quiver.

He took their orders, which they had deciphered as best they could from a menu written in three languages: Korean, Greek and Italian. They asked for a mix of baklava, goat stew (highly recommended) and bean soup, with a bottle of the house red. The food was good and the atmosphere, once they became accustomed to it, was welcoming. They soon fell into conversation again.

The little Buddhist monk, who knew the importance of wives to his own private agenda, turned his attention to Napoleon Chirac's partner, who until then had remained discreetly in the background. Her name was Jacqueline Bloodymary; she appeared to be about the same age as her husband or slightly older, did not dye her hair or wear make-up, and was very French.

Turning towards her with a friendly gesture that signified both 'at last we're going to talk about something interesting', and 'I didn't ask before simply because I was unable to, because your husband took centre stage', he enquired what she did for a living. The pleasant smile she responded with showed she had understood the intention of his gesture. Her satisfaction came not only from the pleasure of having understood this gesture, the intellectual contact that was the basis for civilised interaction, but also from her realisation that there was room (and more) in a person of such reduced dimensions for gestures of such a variety of meanings.

What did she do? was his question. Did she merely collaborate in her husband's work and accompany him on his travels, or did she have her own interests?

Her reply came as a great surprise to him, a rare occurrence as Buddhism usually shielded one against shocks of any kind.

I am a . . . cartoonist.

A cartoonist? She had smiled as she said this, and hesitated a little, as if the word might have more than one meaning. The mysteries of language.

But she had not meant to create an enigma or have him guess what she meant. She explained at once, accentuating her smile – that is, making it look serious.

She drew 'cartoons' for tapestries.

The little Buddhist monk mentally flipped through the folders in his memory archive, and came up as intelligently as ever with:

'Aubusson?'

No, not quite. It was a dream of hers to work one day for the famous tapestry makers, but at the moment she did so for more modest manufacturers, family firms or old village workshops that needed to update their designs. She was aiming for Aubusson, but had no wish to rush her apprenticeship, like a writer who learns to write a novel by writing short stories.

But that must be poetic work, even if it were considered as a stepping-stone towards a more artistic endeavour. Especially since she could never tell what the final outcome would be.

He was right: it was like writing film scripts. What counted was the idea; that was what she was paid for, and she felt like an inventor. In her case, it was a visual idea.

Where did she get her ideas?

Where did she not get them from! At one time she had let her pencil roam over the paper for entire afternoons (endless notebooks) and then chose from this ocean of doodles some short black lines where something new, suggestive or mysterious had been registered.

The little Buddhist monk, raising eyebrows that were themselves short black lines in a suggestive and mysterious drawing, expressed his admiration at the procedure because it appeared so simple.

Really simple! Whoever said work should be hard? It was enough to choose one's work well and then choose the easiest way to do it.

Over time though, she had given up this 'automatic writing', although not entirely: she had moved on to another kind of automatism, that of chance encounters of shapes in the real world, and their faithful reproduction in drawings. Of course, this did not mean she had renounced abstraction, because when these drawings were cut up, inverted or superimposed on one another, they went back to their state as signs suggesting ideas.

After that came a third stage, then a fourth, and a fifth. There were always new ones. The main aim of this change of method was to learn and gradually acquire the capacity to draw the idea directly without any intermediary.

The tapestry weavers repeated this 'idea' endlessly. In fact, for them a single idea could suffice for a lifetime.

Jacqueline had taken a pencil from her bag and had been illustrating her words on the white paper that served as a tablecloth. Joining up all the little doodles with a few skilful strokes, she produced two lines that looked fractal and represented the opposing outlines of the two pagodas, as she had imagined them from the description the little Buddhist monk had given. The space between the two pagodas, ingeniously illustrated, formed the shape of a falling horse.

VI

By the time they left the restaurant it was mid-afternoon. The little Buddhist monk suggested they go straight to the temple on the outskirts of the city, the one he had suggested would be ideal for them to start their work with. Unless they had to return to their hotel first to pick something up . . . No, said Napoleon Chirac, he had all his gear in his backpack, he never left without it. But he was worried about the time. Wouldn't it soon be nightfall? He had to remind him that his method of working was essentially time-consuming as it was the painstaking representation in space of the time it took to complete a 360 degree turn.

The little Buddhist monk dismissed these fears with a decisive wave. He said the Frenchman could never before have found it so easy to perform this turn and capture the suspension of time from the inside. Besides, far from being a waste of time, their little trip was per-fect, since they had any way to wait for the light, the famous Korean light, to become less harsh: by the time they got to the temple it would have reached exactly the right point of velvety density, and from then on would only gain in depth, reaching the summit of the photographic ideal.

He sounded over-optimistic, but said all this with such conviction that it made the French couple want to go and see. And since this was why they had come, and as they had nothing else to do, they followed him.

And so they set off back along the narrow alley-ways, hurrying after the little figure who glided along at ground level. Slightly uneasy, they wondered who exactly they were following. If they had to explain, what would they say? That they had run into the smallest man in the world? Or would they need to say 'the smallest Buddhist monk in the world'? It would be unfair to reduce him to his physical dimensions, because they had been able to appreciate his intellectual and human capabilities, and something like a friendship had grown up between them. They understood him perfectly, and yet in some (indefinable) way his size still gave rise to the doubt: who exactly did they understand so well? How? Following him along these narrow streets, which were a chaotic mixture of East and West, was like following the genie of tourism, an impression only strengthened by the fact that nobody but them seemed to see him.

When they reached the station, which really was very close, they could transfer their attention away from their guide and take a look around. There were so many people heading in so many directions that the little Buddhist monk slowed down, turned towards them and suggested they stick close to each other to avoid getting lost. Was it the rush hour? Here, all hours are rush hours.

The station was an amalgam of the ancient and modern. This is true everywhere, but here it was even more striking because the modern was ultra-modern, with cutting-edge railway technology stuck like a collage on to the ancient. And the ancient was itself very old indeed, dating from the first days of the train, a time when such modes of transport were ultra-modern, too modern to replace the horse.

They found the ticket office. Napoleon Chirac went up to the window; behind a thick pane of glass, an impassive Korean man spoke to him in Korean through a microphone. His discreet lip movements did not coincide with the sounds emerging from the speaker. The Frenchman realised that not only did he not understand him, but that he didn't know what to say to him either, as he had no idea where they had to buy tickets for. From down below came the helpful voice of the little Buddhist monk telling him the name of the station that was their destination. He made him repeat it, because he found the devilish pronunciation of oriental names hard to follow. As he had to look down to perform this short dialogue, the ticket clerk, who could not see below the customer's chest, probably thought he was either consulting the ground itself, or a little dog. Eventually he was able to say the name of the station and held up three fingers to show that he wanted three tickets. At the same time as the clerk said something incomprehensible, the little voice down below shouted: 'No, two! Only two!' A moment of confusion followed, since the Frenchman was obliged to carry on two dialogues at once, so that while he persisted with the incomprehensible station name (varying his pronunciation slightly) and still held up his three fingers, he also said to the figure below him: 'Why two? Aren't you coming with us?' This worried him, as it meant a change of plan. And as more unintelligible words poured from the speaker, the voice below explained that Buddhist monks travelled for free on the Korean railways. So Napoleon began to signal with two fingers, bending the third back into the palm of his hand.

Once the problem had been resolved, they went past a huge number of platforms, from which trains were constantly departing. Some were bullet trains, made of pink metal and aerodynamic in shape; others were old and dilapidated, pulled by steam locomotives.

Theirs was somewhere in between, the carriage walls made of wooden trellis work. But their carriage was quite ordinary, without compartments, and with seats covered in turquoise-coloured plastic.

On board the train, the crush of the platforms was transformed into impeccable order. All the seats were occupied by men in dark suits with briefcases, or women in ironed, brightly-coloured dresses, office workers returning home as smartly dressed as if they were just starting their day.

There was a whistle, and the train pulled out. If the French couple had been hoping to get a panoramic view of the city, they were disappointed, because no sooner had they left the platform than the train entered a long, dark tunnel.

Is this an underground train? they asked, when they saw that the tunnel showed no sign of coming to an end.

The little Buddhist monk replied that they were only crossing the Rocky Wall that separated the upper neighbourhoods of the city from the lower ones.

They closed their eyes, bored at seeing nothing but darkness and drowsy from their meal and the range of emotions and impressions with which the first half of the day had bombarded them.

When they opened their eyes again, they saw they were speeding through chasms, over bridges suspended between vertiginous heights or steep mountainsides, or ledges at dizzying angles. As far as the eye could see – and it could see very far – all of this was part of a vast mountain range dotted with forests, lakes, sunken valleys and tall peaks. In the incessant hairpin bends made by the tracks, they alternately saw the locomotive puffing up an incline, or the guard's van sliding down a descent; on one side a peak rising into the clouds, on the other the tops of centuries-old pines covering a distant valley floor. They became slightly alarmed: weren't they travelling too far? They had understood that the temple they were heading for was on the outskirts of the city . . .

The little Buddhist monk reassured them: not only were they still in the city, but they were not far from the centre. What they could see was a park, a nature reserve.

A park? But it's immense!

He said it wasn't that huge. It appeared more extensive than it was, because of the high mountains and the vertical perspectives.

It was volcanic terrain, which in the remote past had undergone violent folds and transformations.

Civilisation had tamed it, turning it into Sunday afternoon walks in the fresh air, secluded nooks for lovers and backyards for childish antics. A proof of how moderate-sized it was came from the fact that mothers sent their children to play there in the time between coming home from school and the evening meal. When they wanted them to come in, all they had to do was lean out of a window and give a shout. As they gazed out at the vast landscape stretching to the horizon, the French couple could scarcely believe it. They asked what the place was called.

The Mountain Park . . . of Korea, replied the little Buddhist monk, with a slight hesitation that he immediately concealed by pointing out some of the park's attractions: the highest and lowest peaks, the darkest forest, the lightest, the valley of clouds, the deepest lake . . .

Why is there nobody in it?

It must be because of the time of day.

It's a privilege for all these people, said Napoleon Chirac, to come home from work in the evening and to be able to enjoy these majestic surroundings. The soul rejoices at the sight of all this grandeur.

He was about to add something more when an incident distracted him. A gentleman, a typical Korean bureaucrat, who was seated slightly in front of them on the far side of the aisle, suddenly stood up and pulled the white cord that ran beneath the luggage rack. The train braked at once, with a loud screeching sound. The door between their carriage and the one in front opened and the guard came in at a run. He started arguing with the man who had pulled the cord to stop the train. The French couple looked to the little Buddhist monk for an explanation, or at least a translation. Instead of complying, he merely pointed at the carriage window opposite them. Outside, a station platform had appeared. This seemed to them to explain the incident: the passenger must have wanted to get off there, and when he saw that the train was not slowing down, he had pulled the emergency communication cord.

But why then was the guard still trying to convince the passenger with words and gestures that he should not get off the train? In any event, he was unsuccessful: the bureaucrat had clutched his briefcase firmly to him and was striding towards the door, deaf to the other man's exhortations. When they looked out of the window again, the foreigners thought they noticed something strange about the station; not only was it deserted, but it looked too simple, like a makeshift stage set; it even seemed to them translucent. The train pulled out of the station, and they saw that the passenger had indeed disembarked, and was walking along the platform.

The little Buddhist monk gave an irritated sigh. His reaction was enough to dissuade them from asking any further questions.

However, soon afterwards the same thing happened again. This time it was an elderly lady dressed in a parrot-green tailored suit who stopped the train by pulling the cord. The guard appeared once more, there was the same argument, with the same result. Since this time the station had appeared on their side, they got a better view of it, and were convinced it was not real. It must be some kind of hologram. They commented to each other that the projector might be on the carriage roof . . .

The little Buddhist monk interrupted them with another sigh, this time a weary one. It wasn't a projection, or at least not of the kind they were imagining. There was nothing for it but to reveal something he would have preferred to pass over in silence so that they wouldn't think ill of his country; but anyway, it was quite harmless, almost ridiculous. The deception had begun when he told them the name of the park. In full this was: The Mountains of the Witches of Korea. The fact was that, according to popular tradition, this area was inhabited by witches. Of course, nobody had ever seen any, apart from the inevitable few madmen and visionaries, and the witches' questionable existence was only revealed in the effects they produced. These were as gratuitous as they were unpredictable, although over time they had become almost routine. The witches were pranksters; the recurring trick they seemed to love was to take over the mind of a passenger on the train that crossed their domain and induce them, in a hypnotic state, to stop the convoy and get off at some point or other along the route, a point at which there momentarily appeared the semblance of a station that was their illusory 'destination'. After the victim alighted, the station disappeared within a matter of seconds, and so did the hypnotic state, leaving the poor passenger with no other recourse than to walk the rest of the way.

The 'prank' was repeated in exactly the same way on each train. It didn't amuse anyone, except for the 'witches', who apparently never grew tired of it. There were many complaints to the Western Railway, and there had even been lawsuits. The guards had received orders to do everything they could to convince the hypnotised passengers not to get off, apart from using force; and although they never succeeded, they always followed the regulations.

The French couple asked the little Buddhist monk what the rational explanation was for this phenomenon. He shrugged his shoulders. Suggestion, superstition, the 'real dreams' of a nation that lived in dreams, who could say? It might also be some kind of metaphor employed by a population alienated by modern life, alienated by their routine jobs and lengthy working days, to express the boredom of their journeys back home, or their dependence on the cruel chance that ruled the functioning of public transport and city life in general.

This left the French couple pensive. The train continued to climb and descend mountains. In the white and golden distances the world became mist and the mist became world. The blue peaks rose like the boundless borders of a concave landscape.

VII

A red arch framed the entrance to the shrine. Once they had passed beneath it, they had to follow a winding path which rose and fell and was lined by trees and flowering shrubs. Sometimes the vegetation appeared wild and untouched; at others it seemed cultivated by keen gardeners. From the high ground they could spot the roofs of the shrine up ahead. To either side, beyond groves of trees and hedges, they could see meadows, lakes, stands of bamboo and ancient lonely trees that stood like giants on the lookout, as well as an old wall that also rose and fell almost parallel with the path, but now to the left, and now to the right. In the silence, the birdsong was loud and clear, with such a variety of different calls it was as if the birds had gathered from all latitudes and continents for an international competition.

Their guide had been telling the truth when he had said they would not be bothered by tourists, because there were no visitors to be seen. Here and there solitary monks strolled along or stood stock still to contemplate a flower or empty space. They neither greeted nor looked at them, but something about their self-absorption led Napoleon Chirac to think he and his camera might not be welcome. Would the temples even be open to the public?

Wouldn't they need special authorisation to photograph them? He reproached himself for not having asked before. They had touched on so many things in their conversation, and yet this fundamental point had escaped him. Striding along the path in front of them, the little Buddhist monk seemed certain of a good reception, but maybe he took it for granted without having checked. After all, he was a monk, and so it was logical that he should have free access to all the temples he took it into his head to visit. But perhaps he had never been to one accompanied by foreigners.

Well, there was no point creating so many problems for oneself. If they didn't allow him to work, he had not missed much. He could regard it as an agreeable walk that had taught them a lesson. But they would have lost a day. Without being able to explain how it had happened, Napoleon's thoughts had taken a pessimistic turn. The atmosphere of the place continued to suggest that things wouldn't be so easy.

He glanced out of the corner of his eye at Jacqueline. She was walking with obvious delight as she admired

the vegetation, breathing in its perfumes, and doubtless making mental notes for her cartoons. He tried to
copy her carefree attitude and enjoy the moment. It
couldn't be that difficult; all he had to do was recover
the optimistic mood he had been in for most of the day.

However, in order to recover it, did he not first
need to work out what had prompted it? The key obviously lay in their providential encounter with the little
Buddhist monk at the moment they'd stepped outside
their hotel to breathe the air of Korea. Providential in
the extreme: bumping into a native who spoke French,
knew everything, someone they got on with and who
had offered to be their guide. All the problems of a
journey to distant lands had been resolved at a stroke.
Wasn't there something magical about it?

My word, but there was! So why not continue to
trust in that magic? It was very easy to do so, because
it had not been exhausted by their initial encounter.
Napoleon realised there was an extra element that had
made everything even more special, and was still having
its effect: the physical size of the little Buddhist monk.
Something as trivial as an excess in dimensions – in
this case, a negative excess – was enough to suggest
that he was supernaturally effective.

No sooner had Napoleon formulated this reassuring
line of reasoning than he saw something that plunged
him back into confusion. A monk had appeared some

way off at a bend in the path. He was absorbed in the contemplation of a spiderweb. And the fact was that this monk was astonishingly little. The Frenchman's dismay was immediate. If there were other monks this small, the magic of 'his' was lessened. He looked from one to the other. Even if the distance prevented him from properly estimating his size, the newcomer must have been about half as tall as an average man. Of course, this still left him considerably taller than the little Buddhist monk. At the risk of stumbling on the uneven ground, he continued to stare, and it seemed that this monk was even a little bit bigger than he had first calculated. A rapid glance at their mannikin guide reassured him completely: 'theirs' was definitely smaller. He must have been confused by the identical names he applied to them both, because this temple resident was also a 'little Buddhist monk': nobody could deny that he really was small. In addition to being a relative term, 'small' was a very broad term, very 'big' in its own way. And if there was still any doubt as to how correct his estimation was due to the distance, it was a doubt in their monk's favour, because distance makes things smaller.

The tranquillity brought by this reasoning, which passed through his French mind as rapidly as a lightning flash, didn't last long. This was because no sooner had the first monk disappeared from his range of vision than another one appeared, equally immobile and concentrating on some thought or other: and he was much smaller than the previous. Napoleon roughly calculated that he must be half the size, although he did not want to exaggerate: this one was further away from the path and was standing in a hollow, or perhaps on a hillock; it was hard to calculate. Whatever the case, he was strikingly tiny. Was Napoleon to conclude that in Korea the vocation of Buddhist monks was reserved for people of reduced size? If that were so, the sense of enchantment produced upon them by the little Buddhist monk was simply due to their ignorance as foreigners; they would have to rethink the way they had adopted him as a magical spirit or talisman. While considering this, Napoleon looked ahead of him once more and had the pleasant surprise of confirming that 'his' little Buddhist monk was still smaller, like one of those legendary champions whom the new generations of competitors try to surpass but cannot. He screwed up his eyes (but there was no point concentrating hard on this isolated figure, because that only made him seem larger), then quickly turned his head to superimpose his outline on that of the other monk. But this one had disappeared behind a hedge, or perhaps the path had turned a corner.

At that very moment, to complete his mental confusion, he spotted a third little monk also standing lost in meditation (apparently they had nothing better to do), also tiny. Except that he was much smaller; Napoleon thought he was about half as tall as the second one, and the first one now seemed to him enormous. In his bewildered state, he was unable to decide whether this monk was much further off than the previous ones, or much closer. He tried to get a good view of him before looking away, because he suspected that he was going to disappear as soon as he had taken a few more steps, hidden behind a shrub or some such. He did not take long observing him, because he needed to keep an eye on the little Buddhist monk, who was still striding out ahead of them. He was relieved to see yet again that he was still smaller, incomparably smaller. But if new monks from the temple kept appearing who were smaller each time, wouldn't one eventually beat him?

The Frenchman tried to get this stupid game out of his head. He had no idea why he had started it in the first place. What did he care if there were bigger or smaller monks? But it wasn't so simple. Once he had embarked on this speculation, it wasn't easy to return to the starting point and not set off. It might be easier to take the speculation to the opposite extreme, and get out of it that way. He made one last effort in this direction: maybe the monks he had seen were one and the same, seen from varying angles and distances; given the winding nature of the path, this was not such a far-fetched idea. If this were so, it would explain his sensation that, however small they were, they would never be as small as their little Buddhist monk: the reduction in size due to distance is never that deceptive, thanks to the automatic corrections the brain carries out.

Another explanation could be that they were not real monks at all, but statues, like the cement gnomes that people put in their gardens, statues of the temple's ancestral *bodhisattvas* whose different sizes represented their level of importance or illumination. And of course, these two explanations were not mutually exclusive.

Napoleon Chirac recognised that it was childish of him to cling to the belief that his little Buddhist monk was the smallest Buddhist monk in the world, and yet in every artist there is a remnant of childhood not assimilated into the adult personality, like a sea-horse in a human-shaped tank, or like a talisman that allowed him to enter all the temples and take all the photographs he wished.

VIII

His work soon freed him of these sterile fantasies. Despite the particular direction that he had followed within his profession as a photographer, which had more to do with phantoms than realities, the process was a more concrete manipulation of reality. And because he was still uncertain how much time he would have, in spite of the little Buddhist monk's assurances, he set to work with a certain urgency. What a contradiction: he was abandoning a desperate attempt to prove to himself that he had come across someone who could manipulate dimensions as if by magic, only to almost instantaneously reject the assurances about enchanted, suspended time that this same being had made. But this wasn't really a contradiction, or it should be said that realism was a contradiction in itself. The flowers from a lemon tree are not lemony, and yet its leaves are! The less realist a work of art, the more the artist has been obliged to get his hands dirty in the mud of reality.

No one prevented Napoleon Chirac from placing his tripod wherever he wanted, nor the camera on the tripod, or the photoelectric lighting cells all around him. The kind of photography he believed in made it necessary for him to decide first and foremost which the central point was. But before he could do that, he had to work out what circumference most interested him. He let himself be guided by intuition, refined by his practice and rectified by his taste. He had discovered that in nature there was no such thing as a circumference. It was the occasion that created them.

In general he chose a point off-centre, so that the circle would open out. The centre of the temple looked a bit like one of those raised open bandstands common in European parks. It was made of wood painted dark red, with a very low roof and half-surrounded by a balcony supported on slender columns. On one side was the shrine, which was dark apart from a bronze Buddha gleaming at the far end. On the other, a dwarf stone pagoda that did not obstruct the view of the park. And in the background (but it would also be in the photograph) stood the monks' tumbledown dwelling.

Paper decorations hung from all sides of the circular roof. There were more in the entrance to the shrine and inside it, as well as little paper lanterns in the nearby trees. The impression was of an untidy, gaudy children's birthday party. The pop music blaring out of loudspeakers everywhere only added to the sensation.

Is this a day of celebration? he asked the little Buddhist monk.

No, it wasn't. But as is well-known, for Buddhism 'every day is Christmas'.

The paper decorations and the lanterns were of bright, lively colours, mostly red, although the rest of the spectrum was also well represented. Some of them were spherical, and these most resembled the balloons of children's parties; others were shaped like pagodas, flowers or Chinese letters. Most of them though were round or long concertina shapes, clustered together in different-sized bunches; these were what set the overall tone of the decor. They were swaying gently in the breeze, and all looked brand new. Could the monks have so little to do that they spent all their time making them and putting up new ones every day?

The photographer was bewildered. He was unsure whether he had won the lottery or was wasting his time. The old wood from which everything was built and the views in the background of nature both wild and cultivated could not have provided a more striking contrast to this lamentable party atmosphere. But that was what made it exotic.

At least he could not complain about the light, which seemed to him perfect. He looked at the small tablet on which he received the data from the cells he had spread everywhere. The screen showed very strange results. It could have been his fault because, trusting to the subtlety of the Buddhist light, he had employed the smallest cells. Should he have taken into account the fact that in the East the rational mind is augmented by 'illumination'? Well, he told himself, the cells knew more than him. On a molecular level, light cannot be disassociated from colour, which is why shapes became visible in representation, whereas at the cellular level there was a disassociation, and beyond what could be represented there was only 'illumination' as a mental gesture. Small iridescent whirls appeared in the space between the cells. The rivers of shadow flowed like perpetually waving decorative streamers. He had got himself into a real mess. The optical readers were out of control. What could the answer be? Maybe it was the coloured concertinas hanging everywhere that were causing the distortion. The concertinas could be giving off light. What if there were also concertina cells? Perhaps without realising it, he had made an important scientific discovery . . . No, he didn't think so. The situation was still trivial.

IX

He was roused from these thoughts by Jacqueline calling to him. She was looking closely at one of the walls
of the shrine. He went over, accompanied by the little
Buddhist monk, who had been standing silently by
his side watching him at work. His wife pointed out a
bronze plaque set in the wall which had Korean writing
on it. She wanted to know what it said.

The little Buddhist monk translated it into French,
but since it was still largely incomprehensible, he had
to explain that it was a text in praise of a minister's
widow.

How strange, commented Napoleon Chirac, that a
translation should need a translation.

For her part, Jacqueline expressed her admiration
at seeing someone reading so fluently – as their little
friend had just done – a text written in those fiend-
ishly difficult Oriental ideograms. She said that she
could spend her whole life studying them without ever

understanding a thing. (Although she did like drawing them for her tapestries.)

At this, they heard an amused laugh down at floor level. But at first, the short speech the little Buddhist monk embarked on was critical rather than amusing.

Oriental ideograms! he repeated scornfully. What a lack of discernment that innocent expression revealed. As if the Orient were a single exotic whole covering everything. It was no surprise that, if this was their starting point, Westerners needed not only translations of the translations, but translations of the translations of the translations and so on to infinity. And even so, he was afraid that infinity would not be enough for them to understand.

This was especially erroneous in the present instance, because as a matter of fact Korean writing was the simplest in the world. And it was so deliberately. The Korean alphabet, Hangeul, had been created in 1446 during the reign of Sejong during the Joseon dynasty. It had been given the name of Hunminjeongeum, in other words 'The Correct Sounds for the Instruction of the People'. Its promoter, the remarkable King Sejong, had ruled from 1418 to 1450. A great protector of learning, he regretted that his people did not have access to knowledge because of the difficulties of the Chinese characters that were used for writing. He therefore brought together all the scholars of his kingdom, and with their guidance this alphabet was created. At the proclamation of its launch he declared: 'I have invented a series of twenty-eight letters that are very easy to learn, and it is my fervent desire that they serve to increase the happiness of my people.'

Nowadays only twenty-four are used: fourteen consonants and ten vowels. It is a purely hieroglyphic system, which is extremely rare and possibly unique. The stroke representing each consonant imitates the position of the tongue needed to pronounce it. For example, the 'g' is a small right angle, as in the top horizontal line and the right-hand vertical one in the depiction of a rectangle. A simple test suffices to demonstrate that this angle is a faithful representation of the position of the tongue as it pronounces the sound 'g': that is, flat at the front, and then lower at the back. Or take the 'n' sound. This is represented by a little angle that is the opposite of the 'g'; in other words, it is the lower horizontal line and left-hand vertical of the same drawing of a rectangle.

As for the vowels, there are three basic ones. A horizontal line representing the earth, a vertical one representing a standing person, and a little circle representing the sky. (These are not hieroglyphs but mnemotechnic devices).

In writing, these signs are combined from the top, with a consonant and a vowel (and occasionally another consonant) forming a sound, in other words a syllable.

Children learn this alphabet at the age of two or three. Foreigners can get to grips with it in an hour or two, and thanks to its rational nature it is supremely easy to reproduce. Illiteracy is unknown in Korea. At first the alphabet was criticised precisely for being too easy. It was called Achingeul (morning letters) because they could in fact be learnt in a morning; or Amgeul (women's letters).

This is the age-old conflict, still latent in Korea: knowledge for everyone, easy knowledge, as opposed to the Chinese ideograms; popular culture or high culture, television versus art. What distinguishes Korea is that this conflict is found in distinct, opposing concepts of time, what could be seen as different 'poetics' of time.

At this point the little Buddhist monk interrupted his explanations by saying that if they didn't believe him, they should try reading the text on the plaque. Why didn't they read it out loud? All they had to remember was that each sign indicated a position of the tongue and lips.

But they didn't know the language!

What did that matter? They should regard it not as a text but as an instruction manual, a kind of visual Braille.

They did as he suggested, hesitantly at first, then with greater confidence, and within seconds they were reading fluently. Napoleon Chirac realised that the relationship between the signs and the movements of his mouth were equivalent to that between the light and the flashing of the photoelectric cells when he looked at them on the screen.

Jacqueline commented that she now understood the meaning of the text on the plaque. Her husband agreed: it was the same for him. They could see what a vast difference there was between translation and direct reading. It seemed undeniable that translations were no use at all.

One moment though: how could they possibly understand it, when they didn't know Korean? They had only learnt the alphabet, not the language. Were they the same thing?

'I told you it was easy. When something is easy, it is completely easy. But no one believes it. Not even the proof convinces them.'

X

The temple's emptiness had gradually been filling up. From the moment they arrived monks had been discreetly filing in and wandering around absorbed in their arcane duties or prayers. They drew no attention to themselves, and appeared not to pay any to the strangers. This, however, was a false impression, and when the French couple did look at them more closely, they could tell that they were fascinated by the photographer's work and that it was only their timidity which, fortunately, prevented them from approaching the camera, touching it and wanting to look through the viewfinder, like savages. They restricted their curiosity to sideways glances and to repeatedly passing by, pretending to be doing things they were not really doing. After each approach, they hid so that they could continue to watch from a distance, but they must have had little practice at hiding, because they did it ridiculously badly, thinking that a trunk of only ten centimetres in diameter or a stone twenty centimetres high was enough to conceal them. Far from discouraging them, the laughter this produced in the French couple only stimulated them to show their interest more openly, which they did with enchanting smiles and slight bows.

Soon afterwards there was a consultation and all the monks withdrew to one of the buildings, only to reappear a short time later carrying bags, bottles and tablecloths. The little Buddhist monk told the French pair they were being invited to a picnic.

They accepted, although Napoleon Chirac insisted it could not be a very long one, as his work was pressing. A chorus of agreement and more bows: they would never allow themselves to interfere in the work of such a distinguished guest – far from it! And it really was far from it because, rather than being pressing, time adapted to all the interruptions.

They had already laid out the cloths on the floor of the shrine and spread different-sized bowls, glasses and chopsticks on them. They all sat down. The French couple were not altogether surprised to see that all the dishes were plastic, and that the crisps and sweets were from supermarket packets. The only drink was Coca-Cola.

After the first few mouthfuls, Napoleon Chirac felt obliged to give a brief explanation of his intentions and way of working. This produced a wave of polite smiles, and more brief bows. It did not matter whether they had understood or not, because they agreed with everything anyway.

Attracted by the smell of food (if this industrially produced food had a smell), a big black dog had come over. The monks greeted her enthusiastically, stroking her and offering her handfuls of nibbles and sweets which the dog devoured with great delight.

'Aren't they bad for her?'

'She's used to it.'

They filled a bowl with Coca-Cola, and the dog licked it up in seconds, curling and uncurling a huge yellow tongue.

'What an unnatural colour for a tongue!'

'They dye it.'

The unnatural qualities of Firefly (that was the dog's name) went far beyond this. The temple's sacred pet, she displayed elements of shamanism latent in the sophisticated northern Buddhism. The monks left her to roam freely, and she took full advantage of this because she was both inquisitive and sociable. She always came back, however; and indeed, she was always present, as she had demonstrated on this occasion. To avoid problems, once she had had her first litter (five puppies, which had been distributed among the region's faithful) they had taken her to a reputable animal clinic to be neutered. It was a routine operation, in this case carried out without problems. The next day, Firefly returned to the temple and to her roaming. Imagine then the monks' surprise when they saw that male dogs still pursued her as before, and with the same intentions. When they went to the clinic to complain, the vets were as intrigued as they were, and carried out a close examination. No: the operation had been a success; it was impossible for the bitch to be still attracting males because the organs producing the necessary smell had been removed. They even took X-rays to see if by some extraordinary chance Firefly had a second set of glands that had escaped their scalpel. Of course, this was not the case. After the monks' third or fourth visit, one of the vets came to the temple, where he was able to see that the chasing and hounding continued. They gave up, and that was an end of it. The only explanation they could offer was that it must be a 'psychological' case, even though that did not make much sense.

Napoleon Chirac nodded thoughtfully. He said he knew exactly what it was like. Something similar had happened to him many years earlier, when he made his living from taking portraits before he devoted himself to art photography. One lady of whom he had to make a semi-official portrait (she was the lover of his country's president) had insisted on dabbing on perfume before their session, because she said this completely changed the nature of her image. He had dismissed this as either superstition or mania, but was still sufficiently curious to carry out an experiment, and as a result had to admit that she was right.

The same was true of sounds, he added. The ones coming from the speakers at that moment would doubtless modify the images the camera would capture. If he had time, he would take two series of photographs, one with the music and the other without, to show them the difference. If, that is, he added, his kind hosts would agree to switch off the sound system for a while.

He had suggested this out of politeness, in order to make plausible a bargain that he had no intention of honouring. To his surprise, the monks took this very seriously. After glancing at one another to consider it, they replied that no, they did not agree to turn off the music even for a moment. This was accompanied by their constant smiles and bows, repeated on all sides, but their refusal was so categorical and unexpected that the photographer's face must have betrayed his dismay, and so they condescended to offer him an explanation. This was more unexpected yet: without music, the temple was too depressing . . .

How frivolous they were. The presence of the music could not have any ritual function because it was made up of the most vulgar 'top ten' radio hits for teenagers; and if they found the temple depressing, why had they become monks? They didn't seem like real Buddhist monks, or at least not like the conventional image a foreigner might have of their kind. The truth is, there is no reason that a foreigner's conventional idea or prejudice should coincide with reality, and in general it doesn't. During their first day in Korea they had been able to correct some of their misapprehensions, but the little Buddhist monk who was their guide was too small a sample for them to make any sweeping generalisations.

The best way out of this awkward moment was to change topics. The French couple did this, although not completely: they simply went back to the dog, which was still with them. Was she a guard dog? No. There was nothing to guard. But she was very helpful. She pulled the little cart the monks used to go for trips in round the park. This was too large, and its most delightful spots were so far away they would never reach them without the aid of Firefly.

How was this possible? Even though the dog was large, she was not enormous. And the monks were not that diminutive. Another enigma yet to be resolved.

XI

It was true that they were of normal size, but only on the outside; mentally they were like children. They demonstrated this when Napoleon Chirac went back to work, and they started their jokes. Or perhaps they weren't jokes? A cosmopolitan traveller, the Frenchman knew that 'jokes' could easily lead to misunderstandings. If assumptions were different, the humorous could seem serious, and the serious be taken as another token of humour. Often, the lack of understanding between civilisations was nothing more than a gap between the appreciation of a joke. And this mismatch had survived globalisation, which nowadays had converted all civilisations into one. What had replaced extinct exoticism within this unified culture were differences of level: between children and adults, for example, or between low and high culture. However, everything seemed to indicate that these alternatives were one and the same thing, with children, the popular and the humorous on one side, and on the other, the adult, learned and serious.

Looking round him at the monks, Napoleon Chirac wondered about the future of his work. Even if they didn't wager exclusively on posterity, artists always counted on some kind of historical prolongation. But in the period of history into which he had been born, every-thing tended towards the ephemeral. Fed on television, the new generations were not storing up time, without which art did not exist. His photos would need many years to 'mature' and be surrounded by the aura of a lost world which makes a work valuable. And by that time, if things continued in the same direction, the public's taste would have fatally degenerated.

And yet, returning to work after the picnic and before he became aware of the monks' antics, he had felt a frisson of euphoria when he thought of the fleet-ing nature of light. This was a contradiction, although possibly it made sense in the place he found himself in. Here in Korea, the eternal was produced thanks to what was fleeting, and not in spite of it. And the paradox did not end there . . .

This wasn't the first time that his reflections on the artistic process became impossible to communicate, like a vertiginous spiral of silence (or unformulated thoughts). He was left alone, and in his case this meant being separated mentally from his wife. The vertigo inspired by the emptiness of these moments was due to the fact that his marriage was the real story of his life. And the marriage was gradually turning into a dry husk where it was only possible to follow the fossilised remains of the tentacles of the paradox. Paradoxical tentacles. In his youth, he had loved the beautiful Jacqueline Bloodymary madly, when she was a bacteriologist psychically in thrall to the sinister director of her laboratory. After the liberation, they had both chosen the path of art, but it could be said that they had done so from the opposite shores of time: him in the instant of the click of the camera shutter; she in the months, if not years, that it took weavers to complete a tapestry. And yet, for him to reach that click required a great deal of work with space and time, whereas for her, to reach that slow task of weaving she needed only the instant of finding the idea. This contradiction kept them apart. Now as he watched her strolling happily and filled with inspiration among the flowers and birds, he was drowning in a sea of doubts.

Buddhism was becoming increasingly devalued for him. At first he couldn't believe it, but now he had to accept the evidence: the monks were playing jokes on him. They must have understood that his intention was to photograph the circle of the temple empty of people, and were sabotaging his efforts by walking in front of the camera. They didn't do this out of spite, but because they were so childish. And they did it just like small children, pretending not to in a way that fooled no one. Giggling, whispering, glancing at him and making throwaway theatrical gestures whenever he looked at them. Two or three of them would link arms and walk directly in front of the camera, holding back their laughter only for it to burst out moments later when they ran behind a tree to watch the following group's trick or to prepare their own next one. They perfected their manoeuvres with fake excuses, calling to each other from one side to the other, or pretending (clumsily) they had something urgent to tell a colleague, or that they had forgotten something and had to cross again where they had just crossed. Or they sent Firefly: that really amused them. They would throw a stick for her to retrieve, or call her to give her a pat that could not be postponed.

Napoleon Chirac let them get on with it. At first it amused him, but in the end their puerile persistence annoyed him. He did not think the photographs would suffer, because he was keeping the shutter open to take long exposures, so that nothing that moved would be registered. But there was something else, which led him to think they must know more about photography than he had first thought. This shouldn't have astonished him, if many tourists visited the temple. He noticed that their movements as they passed through the field covered by the lens were not regular. They slowed down at particular points which were always the same, although different for each monk. Not only did they slow down, there was a point at which they came to a halt, before which they changed gesture and posture, only to resume the normal ones immediately afterwards and continue on their way, accelerating imperceptibly until they left the circle. This was done so quickly that he was never sure he had seen anything. But it was repeated after a few minutes by the same people in exactly the same spot. Were they pulling a face, or making a comic gesture? If they repeated it sufficiently frequently and were careful enough to do so in exactly the same spot (a millimetric mistake would ruin the effect), in the end they would leave an impression on the photographic film and the image would be full of monks fixed by the same mechanism that should have rendered them invisible. A triumph of coordination, possible only thanks to that kind of inhuman lifelong training in which the Orient specialised. But what a gratuitous, useless triumph! All it could do was to transform movement into immobility, the invisible into the visible, a joke about motion into a joke about seeing. And Firefly had obviously also been trained.

Since the tripod gyrated on its own, Napoleon Chirac had nothing to do, and so fell into a musing that expanded on these recent reflections. To him it seemed as though destiny might also be fixing in grotesque grimaces a life lived at a speed that no emulsion (God's ever-open eye) could capture. And all thanks to small, pointless repetitions.

He felt that his art was fragile, that he himself was fragile, and became so panic-stricken that all these thoughts were driven from his mind.

How often did he have to tell himself that it was better to enjoy the moment and forget his worries? To distance himself and lose himself in what was there, which was substantially more than an instant: a sublime afternoon suspended from the trees, the chirping of the birds, the depths of the stilled breeze. But this was easier to say than do. His anxiety was linked precisely to the instant: that is where it emerged from, and to where it returned.

The concertina lanterns with their painfully bright colours continued to be revealed in the photo, continued to 'appear', while he tried to think and feel and live in time.

XII

In the meantime, Jacqueline Bloodymary had wandered off along the paths in the park. She was used to disappearing when she accompanied her husband on his photographic excursions (and he always insisted she accompany him), because since the images travelled through 360°, there was no place for her. This was how she had ended up with a better knowledge than him of the countries they had visited and had built up a store of sights and anecdotes that enriched her conversation on their return. In her mind, it had also come to symbolise the role of women: 'there was no place for her' in a man's work, even if this work encompassed the entire horizon, or because it did so.

Faithful to his strategy of cultivating the wives, the little Buddhist monk followed her. He surmised that she wanted to talk; he had noticed she had been affected by the story of Firefly. As she had listened, an air of deep sadness had shrouded her features, where until then a smiling, polite calm had been predominant.

He found her sitting on a stone bench behind a small mound. She had been crying, and her tears had dried. With gentlemanly tact, without intruding, he talked about the weather, about the vegetation surrounding them, occasionally slipping in an allusion to the melancholy mood of the time and place, in order to suggest the reason for, without explicitly mentioning it, a depressed state of mind. With a similar intention he sighed now and then, but this sounded strange in such a small person; sighs are things giants do, not dwarves; elephants, not microbes. He said that the coloured lanterns adorning the park were the 'automata of sighs'.

She was not really paying him any attention. She agreed absent-mindedly, and continued to stare off into the distance.

'I'm disturbing you. You prefer to be alone with your thoughts. I'll leave you and go for a stroll.'

'No, no,' replied Jacqueline, coming out of her reverie. 'Please stay. In fact, I need to talk.'

And after a sigh which, given her size, sounded more natural, she asked rhetorically, What woman did not need to talk? Wives were traditionally accused of talking too much, but that was unfair. There were so many silences that accumulated in the life of a married woman, so many unspoken words pressing down on the membranes of sleeplessness . . . In the end, it was like not existing.

But, her diminutive interlocutor insisted, there were other forms of expression. Life itself was expression. And in the case of an artist like her . . .

No! There was no substitute for the proper articulation of language. What was not said with words in well-turned phrases was not said at all. And even when she had cherished the hope that her modest, subordinate artistic endeavour might say something, her husband had been sure to silence her. Why otherwise had he chosen this circular format for his photographs, which encompassed everything and left her stuck in a centre that no one could reach, like one of those spellbound princesses in fairy tales?

She must have anticipated some expression of doubt from the little Buddhist monk because she immediately added that she was putting far too poetic a gloss on a more sordid and much crueller reality. In real life there were no enchanted princesses, only hopes extinguished by routine, by prosaic and gradual deaths. Her marriage now was nothing more than an empty shell. She had no idea why they dragged round the world a fiction that weighed on them like a curse. Out of inertia, convenience, fear? She felt she was wasting the last shreds of her youth next to a man she did not love; a selfish, unhealthy man obsessed by his stupid photographic tricks. If at least he were a true artist! But not even then: she had no vocation for self-sacrifice. She wanted to be herself, whatever that was worth.

But couldn't they rebuild . . . ?

There was nothing to rebuild. There had never been anything. She regretted that she had become this ultra-conventional figure of the wife who once she starts complaining about her husband cannot stop until she has reached the heights of nihilism, but it was true: there had never been love, or spiritual communion, not even good sex. Can you believe, she asked him, that in my whole life I've never had an orgasm?

Somewhat embarrassed, the little Buddhist monk admitted he could believe it.

The story of the black bitch Firefly had affected her through a kind of inter-species recognition. Especially because, above and beyond the easy equivalences, she herself had become the subject of a story that could be told in a drawing-room or a monks' picnic and give rise to sympathetic or mocking comments . . . and then be forgotten. There was nothing memorable about the novel of her life, which anyway she had not written. Who had said that truths could be told through art? That was absurd. What was needed was to learn to talk, and to do it well. The stuff of language was not subordinate to feelings or 'expression'; on the contrary, it was primordial: everything began and ended there. It was like jokes. Let him try telling a joke through tapestries.

'But not all jokes are linguistic.'

'The good ones are.'

What was she doing talking to him about jokes, after the lesson he had given them on the subject? Perhaps for her, he said, the time for jokes had already been and gone; perhaps it would be better to give in to tiredness, to disgust, and forget everything, even her resentment. But it was inevitable that some jokes would remain in suspense, waiting for the punchline (because, since she was not Korean, she put this at the end). Although possibly he should not talk of resignation, or even of acceptance. Reality could do without those gestures, which were mere psychobabble. The biological process was not like traditional Korean jokes; weariness and old age came at the end, not the beginning. It was like the career of those artists who as they approach the finish begin to lose energy and inventiveness, and start doing things in a slapdash way, however they can. After all, a joke that goes on too long is also bound to have a hasty, untidy ending.

XIII

By the time a short sharp whistle indicated that the camera's automatic mechanisms were completing their 360° sweep, the 'blue hour' had arrived in the sky. An intense, deep luminosity filled the air. The birds had fallen silent; the monks had gone off to sleep. This moment, which prolonged itself, was day and night at the same time. A radiant night and a dark day. In the depths of the sanctuary, the fat, bronze Buddha still glowed. Hanging from the edge of the shrine, a drop of Coca-Cola refused to fall, held by its own transparent brilliance, streaked with veins of gold and fiery red, its liquid curves reflecting the near and the far.

Napoleon and Jacqueline dismantled the tripod and picked up the photoelectric cells, wrapped the rolls of negative in black plush and put everything into their backpack. They commented on the session and anticipated a satisfactory outcome.

'But what's become of our little friend?'

The distraction of packing up had led them to lose sight of the little Buddhist monk. They looked for him at their feet, among the columns of the balcony, behind the geraniums that were closing up one by one, under the mushrooms. For a moment they feared they had unwittingly stuffed him in their backpack along with everything else. Eventually, when they looked up, they spotted him in the distance, doing gymnastics on top of a mound. His tiny figure stood out alone, dark but with every detail of his silhouette visible and clear and, whether due to the distance, the undulating terrain or the dim light, it took on a strange monumentality. It might also have been because of the activity he was engaged in. It was plain he was a practised gymnast because of the harmonious precision with which he carried out his routine of bends, stretches and twists. He must do this every day, but today had not had the opportunity until now. They stood fascinated as they gazed at him, thinking: 'How strange he is!' Above all, the colours made the scene unreal. How strange it was . . . Napoleon Chirac attempted to analyse the elements that made up the strangeness of the situation; he realised that throughout the day, caught up in the constant succession of events, he had not thought seriously about what was going on. He had an analytical mind of which he was generally very proud, except for when he forgot to use it. Now, taking advantage of this interval of calm, he set it in motion. Out of a sense of professional respect, the first element he isolated was the light. He had not found any complaint with the light all day, and the vigorous phantom of it that still persisted could have provided a thousand photographers with a living. It was truly sublime, or perfect, or any other laudatory adjective that might be used for this homogeneous glow descending from a homogeneously blue sky, a blue as dark and shiny as a topaz. This admiration for the blue hour that had inspired so many poets and painters had a long history in his own life. He had been privileged to admire it in all latitudes, and it was always the same, although of course he had never seen it illuminate a tiny little man doing gymnastics on a distant hill. A small animated idol who threw no shadow on the ground . . . This last point, which proved to be the key to the enigma, was logical, because the blue hour comes about when the sun has completely set and in the sky there are not even clouds to reflect or concentrate its rays from the far side of the horizon.

The key was hovering close to his awareness, and at that moment crossed the threshold and left him dumbfounded: there had never been a sun in the sky! Throughout their long day of adventures, the sun had been absent. It hadn't been hidden behind clouds or mists: from the morning on, the sky had been clear and bright, the air as sparkling as a diamond.

He told this to Jacqueline in such an anxious rush that at first she did not understand. He had to repeat himself.

Are you sure, Nap?

Fickle as only a woman can be, she had forgotten her resentment and relapsed into the friendly complicity of their years of marriage.

Absolutely sure. I'm never wrong about that kind of thing.

Yes . . . I was thinking something strange was going on.

They whispered together excitedly, not once taking their eyes off the little Buddhist monk.

Why then, she went on, did I feel so hot at times?

At times? So had he! But at others he had been freezing. So had she! Neither of them had mentioned it, in order not to interrupt the flow of conversation that had in fact never been interrupted. The revelations all fell into place. The sun was a tiny glandular nerve centre situated in the rear half of the brain, from where it regulated body temperature; without it, the waves of heat and cold switched back and forth at random . . .

One thing led to another, and their suspicions grew and grew. The little Buddhist monk had led them into a parallel world they had to escape from before it was too late. But how? They didn't think they would be able to find the train station to take them back to the city centre. They had been very rash in allowing themselves to be taken so far, but before that they had been even more rash in trusting everything they were seeing and hearing uncritically, without thinking . . . At that moment, a big black limousine with a French Embassy licence plate pulled up behind them. They had been so involved in their discussion they had not heard it, and anyway its engine was no more than a scarcely audible purr. It had tinted windows. The back door opened and an urgent voice told them to get in. They did so, not forgetting their things.

The deus ex machina who made room for them on the back seat was an extremely elegant and perfumed Frenchman. He immediately ordered the chauffeur to drive off, and then began recriminating with them (as they had done with themselves) for having come so far; it had cost him a lot of hard work to find them. The excused themselves by saying they were not the ones to blame: their guide . . . Your guide! The Frenchman interrupted them scornfully: Yes, that was quite the little guide you picked up! The implicit joke about the monk's size led to a lessening of the tension. Napoleon and Jacqueline both giggled, and suddenly realised they had been repressing the desire to laugh since that morning. Jean-Claude de la Chaumière, Minister of Culture and Inter-Faiths, introduced himself suavely, but with a hint of impatience. It was lucky they had telephoned the consulate before leaving the hotel. They asked how he had managed to find them. Luck, chance, a hunch. The car interior was padded and at a warm, even temperature. The chauffeur wore a red plastic cap and was concentrating on his driving. They were speeding along the narrow park paths, sweeping off the leaves on the peonies that lined the route. The diplomat pressed the tip of his finger against the car window to point something out. The little Buddhist monk was chasing after them through the trees as fast as he could, waving his arms and shouting inaudible words. He did not catch them, and they were soon on the motorway, still picking up speed.

Can you explain, Monsieur de la Chaumière, who that little creature was?

Of course he could, said their saviour. Nothing easier, especially since he had already been obliged to explain it more than once. To start with, the little Buddhist monk was not a human being like them, but a 3-D digital creation. That was so obvious he couldn't understand how they had not realised, although they shouldn't feel too bad about it because they were not the first to be fooled. Like others before them, they had the excuse of having just arrived, desperate for exoticism, credulous and blinded by the illusions of the myth of

Korea. Let this be a lesson to them; now they had been warned, the next time they should be more observant. After all, it was not so hard to spot, because the fake was obvious: first and foremost because of his tiny size, which they must have noticed. And if that were not enough, there was something obviously unfinished about him, which his creators had left as a prototype. Because of contractual and commercial problems, they had broken off their work midway when it was only half completed. Since he was only a 'rough draft', an unpolished version, the creature showed clear traces of the manufacturing process. You had to be either very unobservant or very accommodating not to see this.

The photographer and his wife confessed shamefacedly that they had accepted everything far too easily. How innocent they had been! There was no excuse. But why had he chosen them as victims?

By chance. It could have been anybody else, provided they were European or North American. Foreigners were programmed in the character's memory chip, and this was related to the contractual difficulties he had mentioned. The creators of the Show of the Little Buddhist Monk had thought of it as something they could export in order for it to be economically viable. When they were halfway through their work, they learned of the customs barriers the western countries were raising, under pressure from TV companies and the big studios. And so they had postponed finishing their project until they could discover some loophole they could take advantage of. They were using their pilot model to do this. That was why he was allowed to roam freely, in search of unwary victims. Fortunately, all the consular services had been warned, so that they could act rapidly and things never became too serious.

XIV

Night had fallen, and the little Buddhist monk had been left all alone, far from home. His plan had failed: the birds had flown. With hindsight, he realised he had let his imagination run away with him. How was someone so small and weak going to trap such huge, powerful quarry in his nets? Greater feats had been heard of, but not in cruel reality.

The effort had also taken it out of him. He felt completely exhausted from all the day's tension. He had not been able to take his siestas (because normally he had three, one in mid-morning, one after lunch and the third before supper); he had been on the move the whole time; and in addition, being constantly in company was tiring for him, as he could only relax when he was on his own. Now that this much-needed solitude had arrived, he could not enjoy it because he had gone beyond his limits and every nerve in his body was as taut as a steel cable. The lax muscles could no longer support the weight of this metallic structure. He was weary to the point of collapse, and believed he could no longer stay upright . . .

And yet . . . Not only did he have to stay upright, but to walk and even run. He had to make one last huge effort, one that made it impossible for him to think of resting. The collapse of his strategy in getting close to the foreigners and the consequent pain of failure was no more than a little added anxiety compared to the emergency he still had to face: getting home.

And getting there quickly! There wasn't a second to lose. Time was taking its revenge. All the magical suspensions of the moment that he had used to enchant the French couple were dissolving, leaving only an inflexible, unavoidable horizon.

Between him and home lay a forest that he had to cross on foot. He was not afraid of getting lost (fear did not even enter his mind) because he knew it from memory and could not get lost if he wanted to, even in complete darkness, as it would doubtless be on this occasion. But darkness was never complete for him, because his own body, or possibly its movement, gave off a glow. In reality he was not thinking of the forest or the darkness; his thoughts were limited with absolute insistence to the goal of his journey: his home. He might have said – and would have done had there been anyone to talk to – 'My home is my castle.' And his home was pure light. The correct term would have been 'little home' because of how small and empty it was. In his home there was literally nothing, apart from a television set that was always on at night.

It was the light from that screen, intensified by his sense of urgency, that was guiding him, just as the shooting star had guided the shepherds of myth. In his troubled imagination it became pure light, an endless, saving regard. In fact it was the television that was the reason for his urgency. At ten o'clock sharp, the moment after the end of Children's Scheduling was signalled and some cute little dolls packed the children off to bed with a lullaby, a programme he could not miss was due to begin. He had been waiting weeks for it, and that very morning when he went out it had been uppermost in his mind, to the extent that, even though it was only nine o'clock, he told himself he would just go out for a walk and get a bit of fresh air and then come back quickly so that he would not miss a minute of the programme . . . However, the adventure with the French couple had intervened, and now he was in this dreadful hurry. He could not believe his bad luck, although he had to, because it was his own fault: he had been too reckless, and had allowed improvisation to take over.

Well, no use crying over spilt milk. He didn't waste time lamenting, or allow self-recrimination to paralyse him. He was already in the forest, frantically moving his tiny legs along what he hoped was the straightest line. He knew that 'a thousand-league journey starts with one step', and was taking all the steps he could. He weaved in and out of the trees, skirted bushes, searched for firm support on the roots jutting above ground to launch himself forwards, always forwards. He stumbled and fell, and sometimes rolled over, but nothing could stop him. His one thought was to arrive, to get there in time.

He couldn't even calculate whether he would arrive, because he had no idea how long it took to cross the forest. Although he had often done so, he had never timed himself. Besides, he had no idea what time it was. He did have a wristwatch, but could not see it in the darkness. He tried, raising his arm almost up to his face and attempting to make sure the feeble glow he gave off lit the minuscule dial, but he couldn't see a thing, and didn't want to waste any more time. So he lowered his arm and set off even more rapidly than before. A little further on, and his curiosity got the better of him. He attempted a second time to make out the position of the watch hands. It seemed to him there was only one . . . were they on top of each other, making it ten to ten? But then he thought he could see three hands, or twelve, or none at all. The only thing he could be certain of was that time kept passing inexorably by, and it would soon be ten o'clock, if it wasn't that already. And he was filled with a boundless anxiety at the thought that he might miss the programme, or worse still, that he was missing it at that very moment, because they weren't going to wait for him to show it, at ten . . . ten o'clock sharp . . .

It wasn't just another programme; he had reason to consider it so important. It had been trailed for weeks, and from the moment he heard about it, along with many millions more Koreans, he had been on tenterhooks, waiting for the date and time of its transmission.

The programme involved an incredible novelty, the result of recent advances in design and animation technology. The happy combination of a team of doctors, artists and computer whizz-kids had succeeded in creating a model of the female sexual organs. For the first time in history, this had allowed the exact location of the clitoris to be identified. It was not that the existence of this tiny pleasure spot or its position had been unknown, but the man in the street, the average husband or lover, still had difficulties finding it. This was due to the confusion produced by verbal descriptions of it, a confusion never resolved by the drawings in books illustrating these descriptions. On the contrary: it was the drawings that had ended up making the difficulty impenetrable. The two-dimensional representations had all the well-known limitations, but these became insurmountable when it came to the complex 'empty volumes' of the external area of the female reproductive organ. It did not help that humans had evolved from standing on four legs to becoming bipeds, which meant these volumes were in a position that conventional drawings could not properly depict.

The solid, three-dimensional models that pedagogical ingenuity had come up with, besides being hidden in university lecture theatres or anatomical museums, had been too small and hard to manipulate to fulfil their function . . . Until now, nobody had imagined that the ideal medium for bringing the Good News to the public was television. The 3-D animation, digitalised and driven by a specially developed programme, instantly resolved all the problems of comprehension. TV viewers could take a virtual stroll through this first interior, or 'exterior interior', with all its nooks and crannies, its superimposed concavities and convexities. By identifying with the eye of the camera, they could finally orient themselves and discover once and for all where this elusive little phantom was to be found. And the Korean people were to have the privilege of being the first to know.

Conscious of the importance of sexual pleasure in life, the little Buddhist monk had waited impatiently for the transmission. The contemporary passion for television had finally found an object worthy of the eagerness with which a programme was anticipated. Recalling his own expectation was like being wounded by an arrow of time in the depths of the dark night, and made him even more anxious. There was no way he could miss it! To him it was a life-or-death affair, and he refused to consider whether he was behaving like a child. Wasn't this on the contrary the most adult thing that had ever happened in his life? And there was no question of waiting for the repeat, because there wouldn't be one. The producer had been through a lot just to get permission for this screening. The legal battle had lasted for months, and even now had not been finally resolved: the transmission was going ahead thanks to an injunction that could still be appealed against, as a defiant gesture of 'now or never'. The next day, the Korean newspapers would be full of indignant readers' letters from the usual reactionaries, and the scandal would put so much pressure on the judges that it would be banned forever. Besides, nobody would call for it to be repeated. Why would they, if they had already discovered what they were after? A predictable psychological reaction could come into play: those who already knew the secret (the path to the hidden object) would not want the others to discover it. It did not matter that tens of millions of viewers would have seen the programme; the unique quality of the occasion made the revelation invaluable. They would rub their hands gleefully, telling themselves 'anyone who missed it has missed it forever'. They would be able to gloat at their superiority over these real or virtual losers. And the losers could well be real, as perfectly real as he himself would be if he did not arrive in time.

Had he reached the centre of the forest? He had no way of knowing. All of a sudden he couldn't recognise his surroundings, even if all along he couldn't see a thing. The screen of trees was so thick it seemed almost solid; he groped his way along, rushing up and down on the uneven ground, squeezing his way between two trunks or falling headlong into a bush and kicking out desperately until he freed himself from the suffocating clutch of flowers that were as cold and silky as fish.

Looking up, he could see the topmost foliage as black on black, being whipped around by a wind that did not reach the ground. Turning his head, he could make out the yellowish wake he himself had left behind. He was no longer looking where he put his feet, while at the same time he was paying ever more attention to it. He saw that the ground was rising and remembered, with a sigh of dismay, that there were mountains in the middle of the forest, and that he would have to cross them as well. Mountains that were part of the forest, hidden beneath the trees but still high enough to have ravines, rivers, snowy peaks and dangerous bridges suspended over abysses.

He did not slow down. He would not have done so even if he had remembered there was also an ocean in his way. On the contrary, he tried to go faster, but had reached such an extreme of exhaustion that his legs no longer obeyed him. They were like rubber. The tears of despair coursing down his cheeks were no fuel for his flagging machine. But even in the depths of his paralysis he was still confident of arriving. Of course, the depths were not the surface, and here he was aware of the unassailable distance between the size of the forest and his own small stature. However often he multiplied his tiny footsteps, they were pathetic milli-metres. If only he were not so weary . . .

In one final spasm of hope, he told himself that the subjective component of time might be deceiving him. There were occasions when mental tension, or simple impatience, made what was in fact a minute seem like an hour. Unfortunately this was not the case now. What he was seeing was the evolution of species, and that took more than a minute.

This was not a metaphor: he was really seeing. The faint glow he left in his wake had spread all around him, and the darkness yielded to the dim outlines of a gothic, overloaded nature, which from his point of view looked monumental. The trees were monsters draped in moss and creepers, the flowers opened and closed, nocturnal wasps the size of doves climbed the spiralling shadows; rabbits bigger than he was peeped out of their holes to look at him. His panting sounded fearful in the hooting of owls. His progress became increasingly difficult on the slippery wetness of the soft slopes. And yet he carried on, his chest crushed by the weight of anguish, and in his desire to reach home in time he no longer walked but ran, or tried to run, deep in those unmoving valleys, while the forest continued to cast on him its vast, dark distances.

25 March 2005

'Hail César!' Patti Smith

THE SEAMSTRESS AND THE WIND

César Aira

THE
PROOF

César Aira

Dear readers,

As well as relying on bookshop sales, And Other Stories relies on subscriptions from people like you to tell these other stories – stories that other publishers often consider too risky to take on.

All of our subscribers:

- receive a first-edition copy of each of the books they subscribe to
- are thanked by name at the end of our subscriber-supported books
- receive little extras from us by way of thank you, for example: postcards created by our authors

BECOME A SUBSCRIBER, OR GIVE A SUBSCRIPTION TO A FRIEND

Visit andotherstories.org/subscribe to help make our books happen. You can subscribe to books we're in the process of making. To purchase books we have already published, we urge you to support your local or favourite bookshop and order directly from them – the often unsung heroes of publishing.

OTHER WAYS TO GET INVOLVED

If you'd like to know about upcoming events and reading groups (our foreign language reading groups help us choose books to publish, for example) you can:

- join the mailing list at: andotherstories.org/join-us
- follow us on Twitter: @andothertweets
- join us on Facebook: facebook.com/AndOtherStoriesBooks
- follow our blog: andotherstoriespublishing.tumblr.com